the PERFECT PUMPKIN PIE

Atheneum Books for Young Readers · An imprint of Simon & Schuster Children's Publishing
Division · 1230 Avenue of the Americas · New York, New York 10020 · Copyright © 2005 by
Denys Cazet · All rights reserved, including the right of reproduction in whole or in part in any form.
Book design by Sonia Chaghatzbanian and Polly Kanevsky · The text for this book is set in Lomba.
The illustrations for this book are rendered in watercolor. · Manufactured in China · First Edition
10 9 8 7 6 5 4 3 2 1 · Library of Congress Cataloging-in-Publication Data · Cazet, Denys. · The
perfect pumpkin pie / Denys Cazet.— 1st ed. · p. cm. · "A Richard Jackson Book." · Summary: Mr.
Wilkerson, lover of pie, returns as a ghost on Halloween to demand some good pie from Jack and
his grandmother. · ISBN 0-689-86467-1 (ISBN-13: 978-0-689-86467-4) · [1. Pies—Fiction.
2. Ghosts—Fiction. 3. Halloween—Fiction.] I. Title. · PZ7.C2985Hal 2005 · [E]—dc22 · 2003017086

DENYS CAZET

the PERFECt PUMPKiN PiE

A Richard Jackson Book

Atheneum Books for Young Readers

New York London Sydney Toronto

One Halloween night,
wind stirred the leaves in the
pumpkin patch outside the old Wilkerson house.
Inside the house, Old Man Wilkerson
sat, waiting.

"Hurry up," he grumbled.

Mrs. Wilkerson took a pie out of the
oven and set it down on the table.

"About time," said the old man. He
stared at the pie with his one good
eye. It was a perfect pie, round and
brown as toast.

"Mmmmm," he said. "I does love
a perfect pie."

Mrs. Wilkerson cut a slice of the pie and put it on a small plate. She held the steamy pie under Mr. Wilkerson's nose. "After we pass on," she said in her sweetest voice, "there will be *no more pie*."

"HA!" shouted the old man, grabbing the plate.

"Then I AIN'T GOIN'!"

He stabbed the
pie with his fork.

But just as he raised it
to his mouth, he froze.

"ACK!"
He gasped, and died.

That same night, by the light of the Halloween moon,
Mrs. Wilkerson buried Mr. Wilkerson in the pumpkin patch.

The next day she put the house up for sale and moved away.
She was never heard from again.

Of course, no one ever heard from
Mr. Wilkerson again, either.
He was, after all, dead.

Or was he?

ne Halloween night, a few months after Jack and his grandmother had moved into the old Wilkerson house, something rose out of the pumpkin patch.

"There," said Jack. "See it?"
Grandma looked out the window. "Just a wisp of fog," she said.

"It looks like a ghost," said Jack. "Now it's in the apple orchard."
Grandma took her pie off the windowsill and closed the window.
"I think everyone loves a good pumpkin pie," she said.
"It's coming this way," cried Jack. "Listen!"

The porch steps creaked, and the screen door banged, and an icy wind filled the kitchen.

"It IS a ghost!" Jack gasped.

"Pumpkins, pumpkins,
pumpkin pie!
I must have one
before I die.

It must be round
and brown as toast,
or I'll haunt this house
a hungry ghost.

It must be perfect,
or a ghost I'll stay,
and haunt this house
and never, ever
go awaaaaaaay!"

Grandma put her hands on her hips.

"Oh, stop all that moaning,"
she said to the ghost.
"Sit down and have
some pie."

The ghost pointed
at the pie.

"That pie ain't perfect,
It looks like papier-mâché,
That pie's insultin'
to a pie gourmet.

Why, if I was alive,
I'd have a pie degree.
I'd be a Professor of Pie
with a Ph.P.

I knows me pumpkins,
so's you better comply
and make me a perfect
pumpkin pie."

The ghost whirled and twirled

through the kitchen. Pots fell from the cupboards. Dishes crashed to the floor. The screen door banged and the ghost vanished.

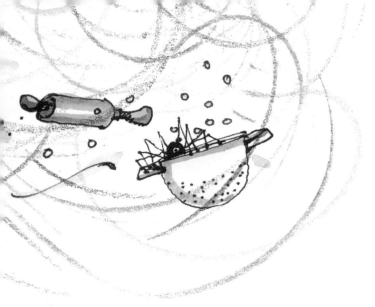

Jack ran to the window. "He's gone!"

"He'll be back!" said Grandma.

"Aren't you afraid?" asked Jack.

"Why?" said Grandma. "He's nothing but cold smoke. He's a ghostly fussbudget with an appetite for a good pie."

"He didn't like your pie," said Jack.

"Well, he better like the next one!" said Grandma. "We'll show the old fuddy-duddy what a perfect pie is all about!"

"We'll make a fuddy-duddy pie," said Jack. "We'll show him!"

When the pie was baked, Grandma took it out of the oven and set it on the windowsill. "Look at that pie," she said. "It's round and brown as toast."

Outside, a wisp of fog rose out of the pumpkin patch.

"He's back!" said Jack. "Listen."

"Pumpkins, pumpkins,
pumpkin pie!
I must have one
before I die.

It must be round
and brown as toast,
or I'll haunt this house
a hungry ghost.

It must be perfect,
or a ghost I'll stay,
and haunt this house,
and never, ever go
awaaaaaaaaaay!"

The porch steps creaked. The screen door banged and an icy wind filled the kitchen.

"Don't you ever knock?" said Grandma, cutting the pie. "Sit down."

He poked the pie.

He smelled the pie.

He tasted the pie.

"Nooooooooooooo," he moaned.

"This pie ain't perfect,
there's things a-missin'.
Pay attention!
Don't you listen?

A pumpkin pie
without whipped cream?
It's enough to make
a dead man scream.

This pie is bland.
It's underdone.
Next time, pleeeeeeease,
MORE
CINNAMON!"

The ghost whirled and twirled

through the kitchen. Pots fell from the cupboard. Dishes crashed to the floor. The screen door banged and the ghost vanished.

Grandma tasted the pie. "You know," she said. "It *could* use a tad more cinnamon."

After Grandma and Jack cleaned up the kitchen, they made another pie. When the pie was baked, Grandma took it out of the oven and set it on the windowsill.

Soon a wisp of fog rose out of the pumpkin patch.

"Pumpkins,
pumpkins,
pumpkin pie!
I must have one
before I die.

It must be round
and brown as—"

"Yeah, yeah," said Grandma, opening the screen door. "We've heard it all before. Sit down and have some pie."

The ghost sat down.

He looked at Jack.

He looked at Grandma.

.He looked at the pie.
His eye grew
bigger than a
Ping-Pong ball.

"Now, *that* is a handsome
pumpkin pie.
Even I can see it
with my ghostly eye.

But looks ain't all,
taste's the measure.
It's the inside that counts.
There's the pleasure.

It's got to be perfect,
a perfect endeavor,
or a ghost I'll stay
and haunt you forever!"

The ghost stabbed the pie with a fork.
He raised the piece to his mouth and
ate it. Then he ate another and another.
Soon the pie was gone.

His eye grew as big as a baseball.

The eye looked
at Jack.

The eye looked
at Grandma.

"Perrrfect,"
he moaned . . . and vanished.

Jack and Grandma went to bed.
Except for Grandma's snoring, the house was quiet.
Outside, the apple orchard cast
long, black shadows in the light of the moon.
The pumpkin patch was still.

Mr. Wilkerson was quiet.
He was, after all, dead.
Really, really dead.

Or was he?

ne Halloween night, Grandma took a pie out of the oven
and set it on the windowsill.

"I hope that's not a pumpkin pie," said Jack. "Remember what happened last year?"

"It's apple pie," said Grandma. "Pumpkin pies attract nothing but trouble."

Jack put two plates on the table.

Grandma took the warm pie off the windowsill. Something moved in the moonlight. A wisp of fog rose in the pumpkin patch.

"Uh-oh," said Grandma.

"Listen," said Jack.

"Apples, apples,
apple pie!
I must have one
before I die.

It must be round
and brown as toast,
or I'll haunt this house
a hungry ghost.

It must be perfect,
or a ghost I'll stay,
and haunt this house
and never, ever
go awaaaaaaaaay!"

Grandma looked at Jack.
Jack looked at Grandma.
"I'll set another plate," said Jack.